PHOTOTAXIS

OLIVIA TAPIERO

Phototaxis

TRANSLATED BY KIT SCHLUTER

NIGHTBOAT BOOKS
NEW YORK

Cover & interior art: Postcards of La Quebrada, Acapulco, México, 1948
Design and typesetting by Kit Schluter
Typeset in Bembo Book MT Std

Cataloging-in-publication data is available
from the Library of Congress

Nightboat Books
New York
www.nightboat.org

for Lucie

CONTENTS

MEAT

No, the fireflies disappeared in the blinding light
of savage projectors: […] overexposed bodies…

GEORGES DIDI-HUBERMAN

Tacked up on telephone poles and the plywood boards that block off the no man's land from the Business District to the Gourmet Sector, flyers all over the city announce the pianist Schultz's return to the stage. They mention neither his disappearance, nor his absence at the Grand Concours, nor how he still attended the cocktail dinner that followed, despite the attack.

Soberly described at first as an assault on culture, the museum's deliberate razing came to be deemed an act of terrorism in light of the minority status of its organizers. The phrase had stuck within the hour, while smoke still plumed from the building: the museum attack, and then, not long after, simply the attack, a term uttered with a grievous shake of the head, which grazed with pleasure on the thought that one could cast oneself as a victim.

Like those of any catastrophe, the overwhelming images of this event churned out in speeches and repetitions quickly lost their impact. The videos in circulation of the artwork's evacuation were marked by an entirely plastic, unsettling texture—more so than even the charred sculptures and empty frames tasseled with shreds of burnt canvas. Carbonized forms, removed by the firemen like pieces of wood while the dumbstruck crowd watched on. That repeatedly aired commentary of an art restaurateur who, in an on-scene interview, explained in quavering tones that we would have to make do from now on with digital copies or the well-known reproductions on posters, placemats, and coffee cups no longer moved anyone at all. The impact had lasted a few minutes; the idea of the impact, a week. It was foremost an economic loss, a vague concern regarding the city's cultural prestige. All other sensitivities were feigned, all other outrage simply diversion, a crusty

3

adornment to conceal the profound and liberating thrill brought on by the spectacle.

The falling man multiplies, telescoping in Schultz's eye.

*

In the public park, silky little bodies crack under the soles of Narr's feet. The sky is black and the ground moist, a sanguine mud. Bits of metal shimmer on the branches of the sickly oaks.

"Public parks are a consolation prize of totalitarianism," Zev once said atop the Jéricho Hotel. "Just space manicured according to political dictate. Their hypocritical purpose is to render city life more bearable, to buffer the riot with the possibility of a walk in the park, the illusion of some bifurcation."

The birds crazed with exhaustion peck at bacon bits, glands, liver, and giblets, while children, running away from those families' chirps, dig and compare their treasures—little bones, meticulously polished molars in the creases of their imperturbable hands. A few viscous crows circle around them. They fly low, and hungrily.

Narr walks toward the pond, that part of the park spared of the steaming flood of animal mash by its lack of sewage drains. There, on the lawn where legal herbicides cover up the diazinon residue, people let their pet dogs run free, destructive bodies hunting the birds that have survived the genocide. On the water's surface, a duck tears out its feathers to the point of drawing blood, curious toddlers ask questions. Across the pond, a military parade—must be commemorating something or other.

The falling man keeps falling, following himself endlessly.

The leaflets announcing Schultz's return litter the ground, soak up the meat juice, the putrid smell of which, combined with the portrait on the upcoming concert's announcement, chisels at Narr like a migraine.

The parade marches on.

*

The course of Théo Schultz's professional life, unusual in the context of the classical scene, to say the least, had by turns been deemed the stuff of prodigy and impostor. According to his detractors, it was all careerism, technical shortcomings, and a restricted musical vocabulary, and the journalists, whether enthusiasts or critics with some other score to settle, devoted entire pages to the young performer's signature sensitivity, the breadth of his palette, and his assiduous stage presence. The truth, of course, lay in some intermediary mediocrity, or at least that's what Théo told himself, the thought as unbearable as it was inevitable. Then came the day of the Grand Concours, but it had already been a long time since anyone had spoken of him, and in the media his absence had been quietly eclipsed by the attack.

On the shores, beached whales bloated with methane explode all over the closing shore shops, their glorious stench seeping under the skin for days. The protests ended a long time ago. Eyeing promotions, diligent guards move on to officially randomized ID checks. Relocated populations bump into each other elsewhere, dismissed by unfamiliar authorities as new arrivals. The ones who stay behind get sick most often, sick like this city whose body's filtration system no longer works, entrails in this air, toxic organs; from now on, everything is visible, and areas that once lay underground now jut out conspicuously. Electric fences, cameras, and motion detectors surveil the unaffected territories, invite transgression. The Conservatory's decor slaps the passersby with its gilding.

Contractually bound, Théo daydreams of distant forests, arctic deserts, and sandy plains. He will have wanted it, however, this execution in the public square. His face peppers the city, ridicule amplified by the public health crisis, the still unexplained overflow of animal flesh that recalls the piano to the bourgeoisie of its origins, folded into the folds of the city.

The audience stirs between the movements, coughs, applauds from time to time. I always enjoyed starting in on a piece before a respectful silence had set in: the listener's guilt over having to interrupt a thing such as art only increases their indulgence. This obviously superficial sympathy is enough for the critics and music lovers, turns into a pleasant murmur that overflows onto the street. To make the audience feel like they're disturbing the music with their noise between the movements is to imply their inferiority, their lack of refinement; it was also a way for me to suggest my complete immersion. I always lowered myself to such schemes, which enlivened my playing without overshadowing it. In the beginning, all of that offered me a kind of transmission, a community, a recognition, and it was total recognition that I was seeking: gratitude and belonging.

You've got nothing to prove, the concert's in eight weeks and the hall's already sold out, it's plain to see they've been waiting for you. As for the fluff, you've absolutely got to talk about how you practice, the hours of practice, the people love work, it sells better than talent, anyway, and you'll notice how artists are always talking about work, even if I admit there's maybe a kind of anxiety behind this word, who cares, practice, practice as work, you've got to talk about it, make no mistake about it, mention sometime how you work on your Schubert, your Brahms, how you work on your trills, your arpeggios, you've absolutely got to talk about it in your interviews, and you've got to say something about all the long hours, too, the discipline, because people don't believe in talent anymore, no one cares about it, it just doesn't work. So, you've got to talk about work and you've got to talk about love, and you've absolutely got to say that one isn't worth a dime without the other, people will just eat that up, you've got to talk about music and the piano, about passion and the nuts and bolts of it, and boom, just like that, you'll have played it well, obviously they'll put a couple portraits of you next to the text, but whatever you do, don't try to recognize yourself in the portraits or the quotes, remember, you're selling a product, just make an image of yourself that's mysterious and accessible all at once, charming and respectable. About all the rest, don't say a word.

Desire is one form of suicide. As with the last glance we shoot out at the crowd, we shoot ourselves with a blank. After this momentum that hinges entirely on a blind spot: the fracas. From now on, all approval will be punitive. Whereas some take aim from one elsewhere to another, adjusting their aim, honing in on passing objects, preparing their consolation, minimizing risk and turning themselves into diverse but modest business venture, Théo Schultz's ambition was voracious and wild, an inarticulate madness. An aestheticization, equally applied and detached, fed his musical staff like his fascination with disaster, ruins swallowed up by plants, forest fires, floods, industrial chemical explosions, snuff films, and above all, infinitely, the image of the falling man.

The scene comes from the day of the attack. Not from the museum in flames but from a distant building, the fifty or so floors of which are occupied by financial offices. We don't see the man as he hits the ground, only his fall, and so the video is more popular than the ones of the Dnipropetrovsk maniacs or the more recent one of Omayra Sánchez's death recorded in real time. Filmed coincidentally by a tourist whose theatrically blasé commentary causes Théo to turn off the sound every time he watches, the video depicts a perfect fall, forever available on the screen.

The witness's distance does not establish their power—if they are protected, the risk they run freezes them back into a jealous revery, a congested longing. The fissure of the gaze is never at rest, but persists in disintegration, imperceptible gaps.

The tab remains open, the image of the falling man repeats, still an erotic mystery to Théo despite the accumulating months, the hundreds of repetitions, his body emptying out as if drugged. He doesn't tell anyone about this. He tries to locate the moment of grace, pauses the video with every passing second, starts it over from the beginning. "I'm twisted, a total sicko," he tells himself, all the while convinced that, in his entire life, he's never seen anything so beautiful.

*

Slowly the water recedes, the infertile land settles and cracks like how a wound heals, a placeless wound—hurled to the borders by displaced bodies—which moves on like blood, uprooted memories.

Narr looks closely at the poster, its use of different fonts, the pieces it announces. She has thought about Théo since the evening of the Grand Concours, it's true, but not until today has she wanted to see him again. Although, it's not so much a desire to see him as a desire to obtain, through his person, news about Zev. Narr decides to go to Théo's. To knock on his door, convinced he still lives in the same apartment: per Schultzian logic, a change of address would have required an update of his promotional photograph.

*

"Théo! It's me. The building's locked, I'm downstairs."

The aggressive buzzing of the intercom vibrates down to Narr's bones. In the vestibule a man mops the tiled floor, muttering under his breath about how his job is pointless, given the pervasive smell and all this dust that has started to creep in. "Better head home, young lady. They say one hell of a storm's coming."

You open the door for me, but I was already open, like a cracked fruit, and you stand there smiling, calm in the doorway, at the threshold, as if you'd spent the last year waiting for me, but I can see you shaking, too, where your collar bones meet, and all of a sudden I want to bite you till you scream, till you bleed, you know I've seen the poster, that's how you explain my presence here, and I can feel your shame, you're ashamed, aren't you?

"Coming in?"

Théo's room oozes a studied dilapidation. Narr knows of his means, that enormous inheritance, knows that behind his bohemian airs, behind these dirty walls and the mattress on the floor, behind the dust and old photos taped up on the doors hides an aristocratic guilt. The objects are all the same as before. Théo repeats himself. Regulation envelops him, an ingested metronome.

"Come on, have a seat."

"I saw what happened... the concert. Bravo."

"Yeah, well, you know..."

"What?"

"Oh, nothing."

They eye each other like animals considering whether the prey is worth the attack.

"Do you need money?"

"Oh, fuck off."

"No, I mean it. What did you come here for? Are you lonely? Do you want something?"

"I don't know... to slap you in the face."

"Why?"

"To get you to come out of your shell a bit."

Théo doesn't ask Narr to leave. He just stands there, looking disgusted and squirming.

Narr scolds him with a half-smile.

"The last time I saw you, you were puking prosciutto all over my rug."

"I already said I'm sorry. I was in a bad place. The Concours, the cocktail party, all those people... But let's be honest: that rug was hideous. I was only doing you a favor."

"I'm not looking for apologies. I'm glad to see you again."

"Me too."

"You seem tired."

"Not as tired as you. It's this war. The city's suffocating, it just never ends…"

"Feel like going for a walk in the park together? Out in the storm."

Outside the dust is rising, slowly reaching the upper stories. Théo closes the window.

"All right. Let's go."

THÉO

I haven't been in touch with Zev since he left for good. I didn't want to cling to him anymore. It was all starting to look like love, but I could feel a despondency coming on, and the thought that he might notice horrified me. I almost wrote to him once, joking around, to forward an article I'd just read. It was called, "Rise in Animal Population in Radioactive Environments." I thought he'd appreciate the picture of the deer, partridges, and boars in Chernobyl, that it might make him smile, but I never hit send. Our friendship had been too beautiful for such a banal gesture, especially after such a long time, and since we'd left off on bad terms.

I looked for him for a long time, looked all over, rushed West through the communes, through the orchards, and begged the field workers for some trace of him, asked around among the fire chasers, those pioneers of devastation and fertile ashes who think of nothing more than the profitability of foraged mushrooms. I caught up with the blockades, the resistance fighters, and I said Zev's name to everyone I met as one might flash a passport, and some were familiar with his ghost, a tale, a trace, nothing more than a disembodied story.

After a brief dance, in which everyone wants to seem like they know more than the rest but don't want to say, they all confess, without a fight, that they know nothing about what Zev is up to and want to know where he is, too. Yes, out west, almost certainly, but Zev knows how to hide his tracks and his hatred is totalizing. Narr speculates that he must have ended up in trafficking, conspiracy: it's all going to blow soon, and the ruins will be pretty. Surely he must be traveling, planning various acts of destruction from a distance. "Maybe the attack..." Théo tosses out the idea. Seeing the fire, he had the immediate feeling that it was a message, a gift meant especially for him.

"Do you actually believe what you're saying?"
"No."

★

The sandstorm spreads in a matter of minutes, engulfing the streets, the buildings, finally blanketing the meat and bringing about a suffocation that comes from something other than that smell. No doubt this will give the impression that things are generally improving. But, by word of mouth, people are already starting to warn each other to move around only on foot. In the public park, silhouettes emerge from the orange mist.

The paths fork.

The falling man keeps falling.

Enough with the cordialities. Your artistry on the piano is laughable, the illusion of refinement, gone the way of all so-called classical music. A sickness. The piano carries its own particular violence, demands interiority, sedentariness, it's the double frontier of execution: the salon on the one hand, the gallows on the other. Don't be fooled, ever since the beginning it's been about distracting us from a revolution that's already underway, keeping little ladies busy and seducing them into their caste. You already know all that, don't you, Théo Schultz? That's why you pulled out of the Grand Concours, that's what you told me at the cocktail party. I saw the fire, you said. If you do come and play here, it's only because you can't, or don't, know how to do anything else. You want to cover up all your embarrassment over being alive. And that's what it means to be a pianist, ever since the old days of patrons. That's it. Go look at the garbagemen, the cleaning ladies, the supermarkets, the traffic jams, go take a walk in the Northern District, or out by the city limits—only then will I let you talk to me of survival. They told you you had talent? They let you hoover up grant money and public funding? Very well. Your job, like mine, is first and foremost to entertain the rich. The old lords. People with horrible taste. So, let's start back in. From measure 17. *Andante!*

PRELUDE

Don't bother trying to walk through walls because,
beyond the walls, there are further walls. The prison goes on
forever. You have to escape through the roofs, toward the sun.

BERNARD-MARIE KOLTÈS

Projected behind the sweat-soaked man at the podium was a photograph of discolored skulls piled on top of each other. The image had been blown up to fill the huge screen and the bones' pixelated edges disrupted the grave solemnity the academic was aiming for as he wrapped up his talk. It didn't address any particular genocide, but genocide as a general concept. While underscoring, in his conclusion, the importance of intellectual gatherings such as this one, he circled back to the concepts of humanity and dialogue, and a laugh broke out in the auditorium after he pronounced the word "dignity," causing a discomfort that expressed itself in a general squirming, as if everyone in the auditorium had simultaneously found themselves afflicted with the same gastrointestinal pain. It wasn't nervous laughter, or forced. It was the laughter of someone who finds something genuinely hilarious.

Taking advantage of the complementary wine and cheese that signalled the conference's end, Narr tossed random piles of brie, goat, and swiss cheese on precut slices of wholegrain baguette, all while discretely slipping rice crackers and dried apricots into the wooly pockets of her coat. Her presence in places like this was motivated above all by her worries over food and, just as she was getting ready to move on to the wine, she saw the man who had laughed, whom she didn't yet know as Zev, or anyone at all. Regardless, she felt she did recognize him, but with a recognition surpassing any name, memory, face, attraction, or geography. A call, rather, of another kind. Sitting on the floor, he dug through

21

his satchel, indifferent to the disapproving looks falling on his person, and to the ambient noise, which mainly consisted of a series of conversations about the relevance of the talks given throughout the day.

Zev used to say it's always a mistake to prolong exciting encounters, that we're better off burning the candle on both ends in order to avoid disappointment. With Narr, this rule was broken. With backpacks full of the wine bottles they had helped themselves to at the reception, they ran through the rain, laughing like little kids. The night ended at Théo's, who was busy preparing for his tour of the Old Country, the first rumblings of the minor glory that was already starting to annihilate him. He greeted Narr, annoyed by the stranger's unwelcome presence.

Théo was openly, comfortably, suicidal, and saw in his threats an existential legitimacy which, however convincing it may have been to Zev, Narr immediately found tedious. There was something elemental in this desire for death he announced repeatedly, flatly, but no one was convinced by his neutral affect and low-key provocations, or the traps he made sure to lay so poorly. His way of eliciting protective reactions revealed—somehow more obscenely than if he had just stated it outright—his childish need for a hug, for an external pressure that might grant him permission to keep on living.

He sat down grouchily at his piano to "work on his Brahms," while Zev sat on the counter and interrogated Narr about her plans. According to him, intervention was necessary, an engagement deeper than peaceful protest yet more refined than random destruction. The important thing was, above all, not to be identified. He knew all the routes, rarer and rarer in the city, that kept you out of the cameras' sight.

All their meetings ended on these words: "Don't get caught."

They always got together at Théo's place, since Zev never wanted to say where he lived, a fact that did not prevent him from organizing both sexual and political gatherings— though the term "political" was never used. In the dim light of Théo's living room, militants in lotus position denounced capital while puffing Big Tobacco cigarettes. Zev addressed them: "The State catches us, puts us on file, and empties us out. The State is what turns us into criminals." He assigned them homework, readings, and then their missions, some harmless and others much riskier. The idea was to proceed incrementally.

Even though she helped organize these meetings, Narr listened on without taking part in the proceedings. Her reticence quickly lent her a certain authority, and the inexplicable complicity with Zev guaranteed her immunity, the role of a strategist. Théo preferred not to get mixed up in these discussions. When the time came for him to practice, he would ask everyone to leave, sparking bitter debates over the ownership of urban space. They would harp on about his privilege, and great crises ensued concerning his "refusal to take part in combat;" Zev always let the insults abound before intervening. Narr never voiced her sympathy for Théo's devotion, as naïve as it was dogged, to music.

Théo was sizing Narr up. Their rare exchanges took place through Zev, and although he almost never spoke to her directly, he didn't hold back the occasional choice word aimed with equal frequency at the shape of her body or her frumpiness. She clashed with these white and muscular bodies prepping for a combat that would never take place and measuring their vigor by friendly fights, which Zev always won, his red face exhausted and dripping sweat over the defeated. Narr watched these scenes, eating gourmet dried sausage, garlic-stuffed olives, organic dark chocolate, and other foods "reclaimed" from the system: they spoke not of theft but, citing Marius Jacob, a restitution that compensated for the beggary of purchase. Through this gesture, the supermarket displays returned to the Earth's cruel freedom in order to be transformed into fruit trees. They were taken by the idea that these pillagings might multiply to avenge the families of the fruit pickers who, in some faraway village down south, were receiving their fair wages.

The worst thing, worse than the ideological tension and venomous insults, was the joy, and the moments that, in spite of everything, were absolute and sincere, bundled up in a serene confidence, which had as their sole purpose the rallying of bodies around the idea of an elect circle sworn to exceptionalism.

*

Zev lamented how people released their anger through misdemeanors, assaults, speeches, open letters, and public forum debates. "What a waste," he'd say, "un gâchis. A total bust that does nothing but bloat our detention centers and strengthen public morale. We need to channel our energy." He would occasionally adopt phrases of the "channel our energy" variety, New Age formulae inherited from his parents, from that atrociously decorated house with its vaguely Mayan objects, incense, and paintings of wolves howling at the moon, that house where his family had moved in the wake of the failure of communal living, after numerous displacements to the east and then to the north, all those attempts to escape the State finally ending in resignation, his father's return to his trade as an engineer and his mother's to the hospitals where she was, by turns, patient and nurse.

Zev had learned to read human emotions and mimic the appropriate reactions, watching the people around him in order to grasp the nuances of spontaneity. He was convinced that his social remove went unnoticed, and his charm, a loophole without which he would have been completely inaccessible, drew on the disarming awkwardness of his performances.

★

Once among the tallest hotels in the city, the Jéricho aimed for a luxury that was easy to blend in with, given the proper clothing, good posture, a limp wrist, and the slightly bothered attitude of someone eager to file a complaint. Its one hundred twenty floors dominated the Business District, a vulgar, electric anthill in the eyes of the excessively rich clientele wandering its pleasantly furnished rooftop, fitted out with an illuminated pool, a full bar, and designer couches.

The challenge, however, beyond simply gaining access to the roof, consisted in climbing up even higher, onto the giant letters of the Hotel that stood atop twelve stainless steel poles. This ascent was emboldened by the bottles of wine Zev had reclaimed. He could blend in anywhere, help himself to whatever he pleased, and leave again without worry of being noticed: his beauty, his whiteness, his transparent and resolute gaze, the confidence of his gait were all the stuff of magic, of enchantment.

Sneaking up the emergency ladders, they reached the highest point. Rejoicing in this anger that served as their meeting place, they transformed into gods, prophets, judges, and dictators, discussing the world to the point of implosion.

"The urban will of a restful nature denotes a cultivation of thought. What we call nature is a foreign time, annihilated by a stubborn unwillingness to listen.

"That's not injustice, much less innocence.

"First, memory must be destroyed. Archives," Zev once said at the summit of the Jéricho Hotel.

The echo of the cry was answered by the impotence of the heights, the grand declarations by a quiet unease, the same blade pressed against their three throats: there they were, mutual hostages, each knowing well that one of them would end up getting cut.

On top of the hotel our rage was also vomit, logorrhea, the refusal of fixity, of biographical notices, of some level of accountability. Naïvely, we longed to be torn to shreds, destitute, impossible to situate, just spoken words tossed into the air by our bodies without history, nameless and sexless, drunk on each other. Phlegmatic, hungry, we sought out the most certain generalities. To sand the world down, to find for it a graspable form, but most of all to destroy, to forget. If the apocalypse were a bringing-to-light, we would let each other go blond under the sun, all curled up together. Our legs dangling high above the city. I thought for a second of letting myself slide off, as if into warm water; it seemed pleasant, easy, like a good way to get out of the tour. I said, "And if we just let ourselves slide off like this?" and Zev started to laugh. He knew I was serious—his laugh was sour, permissive. I looked at the ground, stunned by vertigo, the anticipation of the impact on the parking lot cement.

Go on—jump, already! We've all got to get our kicks somehow. Plus, it'll give us something to look at. A sacrificial offering!

Zev, soldier and tyrant, rises up dogmatically in the name of an idea of nature. In his anger—proportional to past belief, and so, to the deceit he's suffered—he seeks the dictate that will declare him messiah, the foundation upon which he will become God. Zev doesn't play, he seeks. But Théo, submitted to the casket of the piano, found a way to play. He cleared out, within his captivity, a space in which to play. That's what earned him his success, a kind of magic. What Zev had first loved about Théo was this play, because play, Zev said, implies absolute risk. Théo could play until he couldn't play anymore, until he forgot how to play, that is, from the moment someone told him he was playing. Naming the game robbed him of it. That's the price of exposure, the risk of sharing: everything clotted in the act of being identified as someone who plays, who knows how to play. And so he emptied out, stripped of his love of music, of his ability to catch up with it. Every time Théo told the journalists, "I love music, I've always loved music," he was killing music. And this murder, this botched suicide, this sabotage by declaration were committed of sound mind. Freely complicit in his disappearance, he found himself seized by his own hands, his own gestures, his own face, and it all became too much, far too much. Suddenly someone was asking him to explain himself. His only error lay in obeying. Obedience killed play; obedience killed music.

THE FALLING MAN

PHOTOTAXIS, *mass noun*

The bodily movement of a motile organism in response to light,
either towards the source of light (positive phototaxis)
or away from it (negative phototaxis).

THE OXFORD ENGLISH DICTIONARY

Nothing makes its way through the concrete. Soft, sludgy meat rots all along the way to the Conservatory. Even the rats have had their fill; only flies and maggots wriggle around in it. The government, they say, is looking for a solution. The smell has crept its way into every building, and soon, the rainy season: we fear typhus, toxoplasmosis. People in the city only travel the shortest distances possible by car, and swear by canned foods and vacuum-packed tofu—far away, the drained fields go dry.

The menaced population gives in, with an enthusiastic docility, to methodical data collection. Orders, edicts, reports, and curfews circulate with a fluidity that leaves no space for excuses. Infracting bodies disappear unpoetically.

"I really do hope these ministers find some way to stop this," Théo thinks as he goes back to practice. "Otherwise, my audience might not come out."

The livestock born at the beginning of the crisis pile up at the city gates. No one wants them anymore, these chickens and cattle, these caged swine. At night, you can hear their moaning.

I want to get hit, tied up, I want to be bossed around and I want to obey. I want to be punished, controlled, I want to fulfill a purpose, to become a receptacle of dictated desires. I want to respond precisely and become indispensable. I want to hunch forward, lick, suck, spread my orifices. I want clear instructions, a confinement to dissolve me into anonymity. F. offers me this kind of abduction. F. loves me like that, good and punctual. He pours his anger all over me, and with love. Zev was too political, too theoretical; his sexuality was a conceptual experiment. Maybe our excessive intimacy turned me into a prude, but I could never admit to him my desire to be beaten, tortured, excluded. To ask him would have meant to spoil my pleasure, inversing our roles, whereas F. guessed it right away and knew, immediately, who I was. F., my music, my oblivion, I envy your finesse, and you know my regrets. These are your contortions. You lacerate me, insult me, and even my gratitude is garbage to you. When I'm with you I'm nothing but an instrument, a plea. You split me, you play with me, you play me.

"Théo?"

"Narr."

"Are you home?"

"I just got back. But I was going to…"

"I'll bring something to drink. We have to talk."

"Wait, I…"

"Narr?"

★

Théo's door was already open, a cold welcome that was clearly part of his staging.

"I thought you were bringing something to drink."

"I lied."

"It doesn't matter, Narr. It's not a good time. I'm waiting for someone. Things aren't the same anymore. You can't just turn up like this every day. What do you expect? What do you want me to tell you?"

"I want you to listen to me. Zev was too busy surviving to actually exist, so his absence came long before he actually left. If he lives on with us now, it's through the phrases we've fixed into our shame. The fact that he left is what makes him present, and the fact that he left would have meant nothing if we'd also chosen the forest."

"Okay, Narr, so maybe you're right. But not today. I need you to leave. Now."

"Zev left this city because of disappointment, certainty, and accusations, and we just sat there like his amputees, ratifying his condemnation. You stay here out of some exorcism, playing your scales, saying hi to cops, complaining about a war that doesn't even affect you."

"What the hell do you expect me to do? You stuck around, too."

"You have more power than me, and you know it."

Through the window, Théo watches the river, the black water in which he could so easily disappear. Run there, throw himself in and disappear, to be devoured alongside the unclaimed corpses, the suicides, the unidentifiably disfigured bodies, and the butchered dissidents whose limbs, at night, can be discerned by their spectral glow. Those waters can only be gazed on from a long way off.

These storms usually put me in a bad mood, but tonight I'm waiting for F. While I wait, I pumice my skin, file my nails, can't help myself from stopping in front of every window pane, every mirror. I fix my hair compulsively, smooth out my pants. Everything has to be smooth. So I can achieve transparency, like a reel of film, some translucent nitrate. Because, for F., I'm still just an affair, a cinema that only shows previews, an amusing digression, and I make the most of it. With him, I feel the levity that precedes catastrophe. I open to him completely. But he leaves me nothing, not even the shit that gets stuck between his teeth. He's my party, my cathedral, my exquisite little wolf. I love everything about him, every detail, his eyelids, the skin between his toes, the indentation that runs around his ring finger. I give him everything just to watch him cum the way rain trembles. Sometimes we go for walks. If he touches me in public it's only to graze my fingers, to say "hello," as if we had just run into each other. I follow him, let him get ahead of me just to watch him turn around. Tonight we're not going for a walk, the air is unbreathable and I tell myself it's for me, this storm, it's for us. While I wait for F., I examine the apartment, hide my computer, lift and close the piano lid. I hate, exasperate, myself in these states, primed for the slaughter. I get ready as if he were going to show up on time. The guaranteed lateness of his arrival assures my dependence. I only hope he hasn't seen the poster. I hope he still thinks enough of me to come here. When he leaves I'll still be able to taste him, under my skin, in my mouth. I'll feel alive. I'll take out my computer, I'll write to everyone, I'll write absolutely anything just to have someone write back, I'll envy the sick who have something to pass the time, I'll watch the man falling and fall unconscious, too, to dream the bed is breaking, that friendly ghosts are returning to applaud me, as if by some misunderstanding, because for a long time now I've been nothing but a face, reproduced and tossed to the curb.

And to top it all off, you have the gall to show up late! You really think you're something special. I see you, your lazy arrogance, your pride shaking with doubt. The last thing you should think is that I take this dejection of yours as a sign of humility—I just see you spinning your wheels, that's all. Vanity and vapidity. You show up, oblivious to the collapse you yourself have brought about. You're seeking shelter here, begging for asylum and protection, and that's why you're a has-been. You move with your back to the stage, but I don't buy that shyness, that coquettishness of yours for a second. I see your anger trembling. I can smell people like you from a mile away, just a bunch of flashes in the pan.

The storm died down, but tonight the air's still full of sand. In Théo's studio, the windows are still shut. Behind them, attracted by the luminous interior, moths slide in through the slits in the wooden shutters. They thrash against the window in frantic convulsions, regardless of how their bodies fall to tatters.

Some things about it just kill me. Taking planes on tour, smiling humbly whenever I receive a compliment, picking an outfit on the day of an interview, discussing what food I like, testing a concert hall's acoustics, going to bed at a reasonable hour, putting my slippers on or taking them off, finding out F. won't be coming over after all, buying toilet paper, receiving a letter from the city, receiving a letter from a listener, getting recognized on the street, not getting recognized on the street, hearing musicians discuss music, catching myself talking too much, washing my clothes, nodding my head politely during conversations about war or the benefits of yoga, justifying an impulsive absence. I see myself posing like a dope again next to the bust of Chopin, the photographer is doing her job, tells me I look so natural, that the light is perfect, she suggests I move my hands forward, that I cross them, no, just relax them, yes, put one down, just like that, next to the bust, that's amazing, so natural, she repeats, so elegant and so natural, she's bombarding me and I'm standing there with my frozen smile, and she tells me to try and look more thoughtful, to think of music, to think about Chopin, whose bust I want to smash, she tells me to think of something far away, something that makes me happy, so I think of F., I think of F. and how he'll take me when I get home, and she keeps taking pictures, tells me not to blink so much, but the light is right in my eyes, the heat reflecting off the window has me itchy all over, I'm a bug stuck in a trap, an experiment, a plaything of high society, my shirt starts to get wet, in the armpits, at the bottom of my back, it's this mixture of heat and disgust, we're just wrapping up now, she tells me, these are going to be beautiful, we'll choose one or two, you'll see them when the piece comes out, but I'm telling you, they're going to be beautiful, maybe we can even put one in black and white, for a more classic feel, we'll see. Théo. Théo Schultz, prisoner of the syllables that make up my name. A harsh light has me under surveillance, its insufferable brightness hunts me down, I don't have a shadow anymore. I lost my shadow and, with it, Zev. I look out for some dispossession to call my own, but in my mind I keep replaying the prefab thoughts I coughed up to all those journalists eager to hand in a digestible story. I told them things like "we live in complex—but fascinating—times," or "classical music is far from dead." When they left I found myself there, confronted by my mediocrity and catching myself hoping that a clear understanding of my mediocrity would make me a bit less mediocre, but lucidity is also a projector, I can't escape it. I would have liked to be the humble sage whose speech caused everyone to slow down, admired for his awareness that he still has much to learn, but I sold myself out without a second thought. The music made me sick, and I don't have a convalescent's patience. My tradeshow success paralyzed my hands, I'm hungry for a love I can't help but hate. The crowds, the halls all filled to capacity, quickly turned into bothersome punishments. So it isn't modesty but insatiable desire that motivates me. I squandered music. Trampled it, by believing in my mastery. The attack happened just in the nick of time, I couldn't have come up with a more elegant alibi. I only went to the cocktail party so they could ask me why I hadn't shown up at the Grand Concours, to which I comfortably replied: the bombing. So I appeared like a being gifted with a veritable, indeed a political, anchor set down in the world around him. The conductor alone called my bluff. Vanity! I wanted to humiliate the participants with my presence, above all the insufferable Klaus, who had won first prize, that sweaty brute who was always shagging his mane while playing Liszt for an audience of grey-haired geriatrics and a jury moved by its very own presence. By abstaining, I had ceded him my place, but he'd never admit that. He came right over, during the cocktail, to bring me a glass of rosé, establishing what he believed to be some new rapport of dominance, without stopping to think that he too, soon, would be replaced by some other circus animal fresh out of the technique factories. I was reeling with joy, mixing alcohols, guzzling hors d'oeuvres. Prosciutto. Maybe I started screaming. I don't even remember. Everyone was watching me with an astonished sort of pity. In any event... Théo Schultz, disgraced!

All right, so you're not going to answer me… After all the shit you've put me through, I've got to say it's hard for me to believe this. It was already getting ridiculous. But this time, really, this is just impressive. Let me remind you, you're under contract. You're legally responsible to show up, to the rehearsals and to the concert. Who do you think you are, exactly? It's bad for your image, for mine, for the Conservatory's. It's bad for everyone! So I'll say it again: you signed a contract. You can't go and disappear like this. I'm really hoping this is all just one bad joke.

Film's premature exposure to light causes a burn, a deformation conducive to the metamorphosis of the captured image, turned unintelligible.

When he pushes open the blinds, dozens of dead moths swirl around the windowsill, blown out into the air where they hang for a moment before scattering across the city, torn to desiccated bits.

Théo hopes his defenestration will be written up in the music section, rather than tucked away in the miscellanies.

He feels no doubt, but waits a while, hoping that someone, anyone, below will notice him, but no. This invisibility lends him his momentum, a savorless confirmation.

In this exaltation of the void, first there is a feeling of total pleasure, interrupted, just before his heart stops beating in mid-air, by this tumbling body's regret, its flailing, ridiculous limbs.

THE CONSERVATORY SOCIETY
REGRETS TO INFORM YOU
OF A CHANGE
IN ITS FALL SCHEDULE
THÉO SCHULTZ'S CONCERT
HAS BEEN CANCELLED
FOR REASONS BEYOND
OUR UNDERSTANDING,
CONTROL, AND FINANCIAL INTEREST.
NO REFUNDS OFFERED.
THANK YOU.
THE CONSERVATORY SOCIETY.

.

Théo, he didn't kill himself.
He didn't kill himself enough.

You have to kill yourself many times
to be able to live.

A WALK IN THE PARK

The feeble effort of a resistance, and every surface rendered all the more impeccable by the light.

NATHANAËL

Narr.

Narr?

Narr!

Were you asleep? What time is it over there? It's late! What, you think you'll find work by sleeping in? This is how you're going about looking for employment?

(I hate the word "employment." It's an imp, a ploy, a mint to cover up your bad breath.)

Let's go, my little weasel, get up, let's try not to tell lies. I know you, I'm the one who made you. I can hear it in your voice that you were asleep. Hchouma, shame on you! Do you not want to work, or what?

(No, no, absolutely not.)

And your love life? Tell me, do you have a boyfriend?

Still nothing, huh? He'll come along, and he'll be the one, god willing! Everything's fine here. You could give us some updates, you know, every now and then. I'm always the one who calls.

(I don't want to talk to you. I don't want to talk to anyone. Why should we always have to talk?)

Okay, I can see you're feeling talkative today, as usual. You don't miss us? Is that it? I'm only teasing. I'll call you back later. Kisses, darling!

*

And there you have it. My day's wasted, begun before noon, lengthening the sentence I'll have to serve consciously in the big penitentiary. Today, then, I'll have to break time up, imagine some rendezvous, something to look forward to at some precise hour I'll choose at random: it flies by better in bits, like a rough aspirin you swallow in halves. At night, the hours pass more quickly, secretly, they proceed like fluid from the sex and flow all cosmic into my viscous slit while the daylight wears me down, sinks me recklessly into its anesthesia, its tranquil amputations.

Théo envied my resignation, how easily I admitted my complete inability. He struggled, wracked by habit, with the obsession that ultimately broke him.

We were black lights.

I should let Zev know, it's a good excuse to write him. In front of the screen, I wonder if the address is still valid. Oh, well. I write: Théo is dead. He let himself slide off. I add: Finally. I erase it, leaving the first sentence. I write: With love, Narr. I erase it. Théo is dead, he let himself slide off. I hit send.

Maybe I'll go to the park today, follow the path of our last walk together, just the other day, as a way to avoid the funeral where they'll deliver, I'm sure, their deeply felt, tremulous speeches, chock full of lies, memories patched with plaster like a renovated building. No, I won't "put in an appearance."

I try to go back to sleep, imagine myself in a coma or even dead, run down by a tractor, but nothing works. I can still hear my mom's voice rattling around inside me like a fly in a jar, repeating my name, shriller and shriller. Narr NARR NARR. I hadn't even stopped crying before they wiped me down, imposed this name, a number, a certificate, a plastic crib, a bonnet made in some dark factory, the color of whose fabric corresponded to my assigned gender. I should consider myself lucky: soon they'll be implanting this type of identification under the skin, and at least I can still dream of escape. Mudflats. For, after the great circus of birth, that's when they demand that I live. They empty out my organs, force feed me commands, in order to make me recognizable. Around me, I see nothing more than the requisite docility. They proclaim their adulthood, their profession, their freedom of slaves as soon as they've chosen their corner of the cage. Question capital and they accuse you of luxurious idleness. And even when I keel over and die they won't leave me the fuck alone, no, there will still be locked-door mysteries, procedures, forms, and formulations, they'll shut my dead body away in some airtight box, some urn or coffin, God forbid it might decompose, to ensure it's well accommodated, separated, and this separation isn't only legally required, but valorized: loads of people save up their money just to make it more impressive.

I should have been a street cat, a creeping plant, a crustacean, empty-headed, madness at the helm. Life doesn't cut it for me: soon I'll build up the courage to get out of here, far from these roads, these humans, take the last train, walk out to some far shore, that's my plan, everyone has a plan, accomplishments to tell other people about, to be all fulfilled without seeming like it, they act like it's normal, it should be normal, with their oblique jealousy they sing in praise of the well-adjusted life, exercise, work, leisure, but we're all prisoners here, in these neighborhoods where there's nothing, where there's everything, this existence is accessible, some people have kids just to feel less alone, they lie to the kids, and the kids repeat it all, the kids practice, train, they have their screens, every last one of them with a screen, activities, and soon they'll be forcing the kids to have projects, commitments, weekends, seaside vacations, walks through the country, playdates, a civil efficiency.

Slaves!

Free the dogs!

Burn the newspapers!

What we need is one great, collective suicide. My voice is growing hoarse from all this anger. My body is cupidity itself, falling apart, already cracking. A pierced horizon I demand, neither accept nor reject: I break down, I absorb, and I shit. Existing only on contact, as a plague exists only in its slaughters, but soon, soon I'll get out to the mudflats, out where the word "here" will have lost its footing.

I'm probably a terrorist. Terrorist means being without, a chaos of dust attacking a cleansing, defined by some structure as a contrary element. Those who unveil a name, stake claim on a cause, and bandy about their outrage are no better than clumsy. Terror, the real kind, is illegible, unrecognizable. Already, I can feel my hatred compartmentalizing:

Terrorism is the other's violence.

Terrorism is a refused translation.

Terrorism is what cannot be known.

Terrorism is a word used by victims who enjoy the luxury of not having to take part.

Humanism is a thief's luxury.

Pacifism is a kind of terrorism.

Innocence is always a lie.

Dogs bark when they smell strangers.

Dogs get bored in apartments.

Dogs piss on carpets.

When dogs bite, we put them down.

We incinerate dogs in group ovens.

We keep the photos; we mourn the dogs.

We adopt other dogs when we get bored at home.

Pets are a symptom of a terrorism that precedes us.

We are pets.

We have our bowls, our litters, our little territories, our training sessions, our walks on leashes.

Terrorism is a disruption.

Terrorism is the concept of a disruption.

Exposure is a condition of terrorism's survival.

I prefer the night. The brooded-over descriptions, the solidarity gatherings that give citizens the impression that they're taking part in something, the candles lit around the scenes of tragic events inject an orgasmic sense of urgency and war into a spectacle in which it's impossible to tell the victim from the assailant: every body, hereafter swept up in the illusion of its combativeness, its resistance, finds a place to shout, a direction to spit in, to harden, a moral and lucrative doping where one can finally ease the idea of a role, an assembly. Witnesses climax over the event to which they submit.

It isn't the same over there in the colonies: the recurrent suicide attacks, the relative predictability of explosions and collapses create a resilience, a glossy tint, indifference to shock. In the gaze of trenches, as in that of debris, the lack of anchoring seems like a rapture, an absence too felt to be lived as deliverance.

Sleep off your hatred, quit struggling. The tides are already rising, bloated with dynamic frameworks, organizations to incorporate, career plans, and human resources. I'm not Zev. I'm too craven for a life that would correspond, as they say, to my values. So much rage against the very idea of value; value's the last thing I want to hear about. Just directions, it goes off in every direction, it's already skidding out of control, it seeps out all over, I spin, I turn around, I get tired, I feel them, there, outside, as soon as I open my mouth they'll ask me where I come from, and

I'll have to explain to them how I only barely exist, I'm barely lost, nothing to lose, they'll say. They'll invite me to their table, ask me to keep my composure, and I'll cough up everything I know before my body drips between the cutlery, then into the entangled cities, with the dogs, the guardrails, the sewers.

They'll talk to me of integration, but I'll still be the foreigner. Even the ones who integrate remain foreigners, integrated foreigners. I have my foreign tongue, foreign skin, it explodes, flies out at you. They're always going to ask me where I'm coming from, where I'm going, since when, and for how long. They'll speak to me informally, the better to place me, but they'll never ask me: where are you now? And that's fine, they don't know where they are, either. They run, like chickens, like trucks. Don't blame them. They'll always tell me there are still bonuses, paid leaves, insurance, rewards, and to all that I'll say: no. You've got to commit, they'll tell me, you've got to be optimistic, you've got to take action, sell out a little, take your time. You've got to survive, feed yourself, get dressed, protect yourself from the elements. Bah. Let them condemn me, let them shut me away for premeditated abstraction. If I keep following that path, my neurons will eventually crumble, giving way like viaducts; I'm waiting for the aleatory fall from grace, for my last judgment, for a meteorite to land comfortably on my head.

Rent soon and I don't have any money or the guts to borrow any, knowing I wouldn't be able to pay it back. Paying back, always paying back, paying back pennies, even in conversation. Every relationship is a grift, a transaction where all parties get conned. The dice have been weighted from the very amnion. I could take a train, leave some

Tuesday or Wednesday in the middle of the afternoon, when no one's leaving, go nowhere, when the cars are empty and the transit authority wouldn't bother wasting a salary on checking tickets. A train, maybe a ferry. That would be a start.

My blinding aggravation suggests an imperative. Nothing arrives, nothing happens, I flit around, forbidden, capricious, begging for some reverberation to dazzle me. Erosion, irritation presume an encounter, an intervention, but I can't find them. Hollowed out, dissipated, I'm looking for an inhalation, to snap my fingers, hit my bones, yell at the cars from deep in my bed, to try and become an instigating element, but nothing works.

And yet there must be something of interest. They say that all you have to do is keep your eyes open, that it's a question of attention, of education, maybe, a capacity for astonishment. I could learn languages, the names of flowers, a handful of geographies, there's all of history, too, economics, cinema, and then, well, there's ornithology, the cosmos, of course, and robotics, medicine, and all the ways everything can be put together, but all that bores me to tears. Let them go extract their gas from deep within the cores of asteroids, let them go find the densest way to pack who knows what, let them tell me about the reproductive system of red-headed vultures, of armadillos, or the space-time dilation caused by black holes, let them talk to me about agriculture, fashion, geology, or Mesopotamian rituals. It's all the same to me.

From upstairs, I can already hear my neighbor and her son fighting over his homework. She's screaming: "the Ottoman Empire!" "Greco-Roman heritage!" "Traditional arts and crafts!" "The elephants of the Persian army!" Plates are shattering and the young teenager's acts of resistance are getting louder and louder. The mother storms out, slams the door behind her, and stomps down the stairs. One day this young man will devour his mother, I'll see her blood mixed with blue ink seeping down through my ceiling, and I'll have to call the landlord to come clean up the damage. For now, the sound of machine guns, explosions, and the rattling of a joystick, "We need your help, soldier. Report to base."

From the street the drills riddle me, their twitchy racket is a whole other war, they're widening the road, renovating the façade of the block across the street, all day, all year, for centuries the workers will keep breaking the stone apart until there's nothing left to break, and then they'll topple what they've built, they'll start over, make it all better, that's what they call progress. I don't even want to move. Despite these paper-thin walls, I'd rather let myself grow used to the sound than go and desire a larger space, empty and isolated, so I make do with being here, guessing at the lives of others from the clues that seep through the walls, feeling the pulse of this city that stretches on forever. I am a seismograph, sensing the impending fissures and anticipating the risk of collision in a crowd of bodies steering clear of one another.

Finally, I get up, massive and heavy-blooded. No medication today, never any medication again. I'll be my own healer. I hit the switch. Nothing, gone out. I open the window: the oppressive smell of meat besets me, an organic familiarity, almost reassuring.

The shattering vigor of revolts are far away, my expired brain is ready for the pavement. With my feet all dirty, feeling disheveled, I eat the leftovers: bread crusts, a tomato. To hurl myself against the concrete, concrète, pavement.

Go out, yes, the park. Difficult to pull myself away from my linearity, a sort of dance would be better, or passing through gusts of wind, forgetting, disentangling myself from my surroundings. I should talk to someone. Talking helps you find equilibrium, balance, so I should talk to someone, to no one in particular, or perhaps, precisely, to someone. I hope I'd say: "Come here, calm down, come sit down, don't run away, I get it, I understand your fear." Because it's not only anger, but fear too, that unites us. Fear may be a desire to live, it must be somewhere, this desire, maybe in the throat, or under the taut skin between the breasts. I'll say: it's not required to go anywhere, I'm talking, that's all, it's not even an appeal, it doesn't even have to exist. Breathe, breathe with me. Whatever.

I walk out the door and grab my keys, even if I won't lock the door. It's solid, a key, like a pebble to hold in your palm. It's almost healing, because we'll need healing. Everybody, hidden, recovers somehow from their wounds. That's what they say. And then, shit. The train, the mudflats, it's pointless, won't be possible. Solution, dissolution, I don't know, there's nothing to know. Nothing to see, as they say. Move along now.

*

A walk: stroll, sap, a failure before it's begun. Still embedded. Should I speed up, or slow down?

Here, acting as if everything were normal, we avoid the scum from the slaughterhouse. A man comes up to me, and shows me a picture on his phone of his daughter in a pink corset and a lavender-colored skirt, posing in front of a curtain of pearls, her hand on her hip. He asks me if I'm hungry, tells me, without waiting for an answer, to stay still, and comes back holding a blue plastic bag with something like fifteen dead sparrows inside it with their eyes gouged out. For a second I'm absorbed by these empty eye sockets staring back at me, by the gentleness I sense in these bodies I wouldn't dare caress.

I keep walking and find myself in the swelter of my childhood streets, confronted by goat heads stuck on hooks, flayed meat covered in wasps. Back there, to build up the customers' confidence, they never concealed the resemblance between the animal and its carcass, in fact they sold this continuity, to indicate the honest work of the livestock farmers and butchers. After the war, which some called the intervention, this kind of activity was declared illegal.

Should I, in order to free myself from the lineages that crush me, choose a place, some affiliation? Or would such repatriation mean playing into the conqueror's game? Do I have to seek out a certain memory to reform, is it my turn to carry what claims to belong to me? I'm tired of these strategies in thrall, these city names, these upheavals. Could I not simply arrive from nowhere, free and bloodless? It strikes me they only want a body to put on file. Even dogs sniff each other out, even dogs howl when something passes through their territory. Species stick together to survive, and acceptance never comes without a cost. I don't want to pay the price. I claim nothing as my own, am suspicious of solidarities, specificities from which it would be possible to extract decodable stakes. So it's my own fault if I'm always letting them speak over me.

The increasingly airtight walls close in again, the planet shrinks, they declare victory. All this is nothing more than a transfer of weight. Migrant desires fall down over the next generations, heirs sagging under the weight that begat them, failures woven deep within their bodies. We are the hostages, the ones who surrendered. I'm not afraid of my family, I don't owe them a thing except this anger over their having gambled on me. Cost: integration. A sacrifice, they said, to push me to pick the fruit, to make me real despite all the teeth sunken into the rotting breast of this crisscrossed world a thousand times evacuated, an enormous parking lot, a park of old oil pipelines, roadside fried chicken.

I burned memory. Burned every book, with my body undone, as a tree returns to the sea. Everything blended together, the façades, the turnstiles, the traffic jams, the nursing homes, the fevers, while the corpses heap on the verdict of the night. Crime. My face peels off, unsure what war it comes from. Maybe that doesn't matter. Long distance. A boat, lights pulling away. Some women helping those in flight through the barbed wire fences. They pushed me across, their two hands against my back. I tripped, I forgot. Histories, religions, mix together. Yielded. My body doesn't belong to me. My skin darkens, reminds me of something unknown. Can you forget something you never knew? Documented, undocumented. Official photo. Name, date, sex. Compulsory fields left blank, incomplete file.

For a long time I've been jealous of the disappearance of a little girl who got swept out to sea back in the colony. Since it all happened, I've often dreamt from her perspective, the shore and the shouting moving away from her, the salt water in her nostrils, the sun between her eyelashes, the straining, and then the relaxation into abandon, the marine depths where I see myself drifting into the darkness as the falling man falls into the unknown.

Mudflats.

No.

My fall doesn't enjoy the same advantages as dance: it is measured by concrete, violated grounds, mute entrails.

*

Today in the park the gardeners are watering the flowers, washing the dust off the oaks leaf by leaf because the rain hasn't come yet. A man reads a newspaper on a bench: on the last page, there's Théo falling. What do they expect from him, from the falling man, what do they look for in him, what has their gaze robbed him of?

Théo fell.

Obviously there are pictures, there are shots of it everywhere, freeze frames, captures.

Théo, falling.

Théo, falling again. And again.

There's no point in asking why we watch the falling man. We'll always watch the falling man.

The motion, black and white, grainy, of the first man to have his fall recorded from the top of the Eiffel Tower, then the photograph of the man who fell, his body straight, upside down, from one of the Towers. We try to read something in the image of the falling man.

It's not a question of biographical particularities, of some presumed identity of the falling body. It's a fall that liberates us through our gaze.

We feel a weightlessness while we watch the falling man.

His fall is every gaze's own.

It's not a question of curiosity, of perversity.

Something else unfolds over its course.

Something that can't be measured in his momentum or the impact, but in the gap between.

Maybe Icarus wanted to fall, was drunk on this very desire.

To leave everything behind, to submit the body to unpredictable forces.

Like drowning at sea. The current takes us, snakes around our arms, legs, turns us into trash.

There's a kind of fall there, too, a kind of expulsion.

It's not a question of motive, nor of investigation, nor of the meat we become the moment we hit the ground, the moment our lungs fill with water.

It's not a question of any grace whatsoever, of such and such a distance.

Something hides away, something we'll never be able to see or name.

It's not a question of the moment during which we watch the falling man, but of what the repetition of this image is composed of.

Théo, falling.

Théo's image, falling.

I trip on a headless pigeon. The head is nowhere to be found—must have blended into the rest.

★

On the street corner, people are obviously worried about something. A little shop there, "La Nostalgique" is both a newspaper stand, probably the last in the world, and a hot dog vendor—the idea being, I guess, that you could leaf through the news while enjoying your sausage.

The smell isn't terrible, and beside the steam a shameful line has formed, despite what's now being referred to as the meat crisis. I go up, take a newspaper and run away without paying. Behind me they're all shouting, which makes it a little more fulfilling. What a joy, to run! I'd love to run, forever, until I collapsed.

Far off, the buzzing drones. Far off, the ruins, the famines, the persecutions, and it's all for the best, builds up populations with something to dream about, something to flee, a vector. I envy their discomfort, a source of jolts and revelations.

By the time I crossed the park I'd hardly noticed I ever entered it, and I'm already elsewhere, among empty castles polished by maids, shadows darting between heavy curtains. Back in the colony everyone had a maid, always darker-skinned than oneself, and they'd say the job helped them out, those poor women who didn't know how to read or write. How I'd like to write a Hymn to the Help, or for there to be an All Maids Day. But no, national holidays are consolations, so instead they celebrate Women's Day, they celebrate Refugee Day, the Day Against Thirst. They're like the Olympics; they last their allotted time.

Swerve: springtime suddenly, garage sales and law-abiding lawns. We've been such excellent parasites of our surroundings that we've become their hosts. The expanding oak roots threaten the houses, and so we have to kill off the oaks to maintain our position, since value is measured in the strength of our borders—thus the prosperity of departments, ministries, extermination services.

It must be the late afternoon. The dogwalkers are already making their rounds and the kids are home from school, practicing their flutes, violins, pianos, their hesitant scales overlapping: the taming hour. He came from these streets, the supermarket shooter, twelve dead and thirty wounded. Autistic, they said, or was that another one of them? Doesn't matter, we profiled him, found the victims innocent, we said: they were good people, normal people, let's not talk about it anymore. Théo, as well, came from there, he must have spent his weekends in a salon, on a bench, facing an instrument, that's what killed him, in the end, the living room. Maybe he had a maid as well, too late to ask him, but, yes, I imagine the Schultzian irritation, the sonatas and mazurkas faltering over a vacuum cleaner's hisp, and worse yet, over the gaze of the woman who, not quite as invisible as he would have liked her to be, owned a copy of the key.

On the Geschäfte Platz, between the Meatpacking District and the Sahet al-Shouhada, speakers cough up a piece of chamber music that disintegrates into a light dissonance, probably because of their low quality parts. Surely everything is preparing for a change. I try to remember what day it is, to find some indication of the holiday that would explain this music, but no, no clue, only a slightly reduced population density. From the window of a building decorated with gargoyles, I notice a partially defeathered macaw staring down at me from the second floor with lusterless eyes.

I like going into the empty shops and giving false hope to the people selling sponges and healing stones, sitting in an empty restaurant, reading the menu, and leaving, or trying on, in some failing clothes shop, items I only occasionally return before walking back out. With food it's trickier. I feel like they keep a closer eye on me in the supermarkets, the grocery stores, where the employees risk losing their jobs if they don't catch the shoplifters. However, in the sleepy little shops, the ones in the fast lane to bankruptcy, it's as if the owners had no interest in defending their knickknacks; they're often in the same position as me, I'm less threatening to them, they wouldn't suspect such betrayal from someone such as myself. I end up with a few things in my pockets: a magnet shaped like a coffee mug, a bar of chocolate, a plastic bracelet, a sweet scented candle, a rubber keyring, and some balm that promises long-lasting erections.

A vibration: Zev got back to me. An anarcho-primitivist constantly refreshing his inbox. Hunter-gatherer wifi. Click here. This message will self-destruct after being opened. "Narr. I know. He wrote me just before, he still had his show to play, didn't he? He wrote me: 'I'm ready to slide off now.' I'd like to think that fall, like the impulse that got him there, came of his own free will. He used to say that, in cinema, the cutting room floor is covered with offcuts, the sequences that weren't chosen at the moment of editing. Film or cut time, abandoned. Seems to me like the film of Théo would be made with those sorts of extractions, torn from their movement. Did you see the picture? Spectacular, isn't it?"

The picture is right there, greasy in my pocket: Théo falling.

I answer Zev: "Spectacular, yeah."

*

On this continent, I had two friends: Théo and Zev. The cage and the forest.

Théo, the performer with mangled hands. The colonial ivory of the keys lingers in the memory of the laminated, varnished wood that has come to replace it. A sophisticated barbarism, embedded in the very word "barbarism:"

66

bar-bar, that which we don't understand, which clashes with overly situated ears.

I bend over to pick up the residue of broken stones at the sculpture's foot. I emerge from a music in ruins, from shards that exceed every constitution, from a failed premise, an aphonic gesture. It would take dismembering every formation. Destroying architecture, to find a voice.

Zev would say: "You don't take anything seriously. The distance will end up killing you. For me, this world is made of blood, squandered bullets, camaraderie. And you, you'll never take part in the combat. As if the end of the world only affected ghosts and not living, breathing people. You're disembodied down to the bone, down to the very kernel of your hatred. You're far away, Narr, you see everything from so far away. Your skin, your sex aren't protests. Don't let yourself get seduced by the idea of your mutiny."

Too great a distance. It wasn't long before I was far away, it's true, beyond the point of reference and interferences by which such a point could be established, beyond the place and the horizon it allows for. This distance remains irreducible, impassible; I feel it, solid in my belly, in the thickening that prevents me from being passed through, in the forgetting that only temporarily staves off madness. Every collision is dampened; stab me—it wouldn't make any difference at all.

★

Zev writes to me about his hunt, a deer he killed the night before with a rifle. The shot rings out. Zev writes to me about the blood on his hands, on his clothes, how the corpse smells while it's still warm. He talks to me about his communion with the animal. I hear the gunshot. Zev writes to me about the deer's collapsing lungs, the sadness he feels when he sees the animal's half-closed eye, and his joy in being able to tell me about this hunt, how he captured the body and the shadow it cast as he carried it, the two of them blending together, monstrous in the twilight. He tells me that hunters used to tell the tales of their catches, that it was a way for them to pay their prey respects, to cleanse themselves, to establish a connection between life and death. That the storytelling was a form of recognition for life turned into meat.

I'm dubious about this story, which has something proud and written-for-piano about it. The rifle is cowardice. I write to him about this cowardice, accuse him of it. He answers that he's always preferred rifles to arrows, that it's always been that way, ever since he was a kid. He hasn't changed, after all: he looks for strength, he looks to dominate and, in doing so, contradicts his entire critique, his rage, his engagements against what he calls the System, because it's the System that allows him to kill with such certainty.

The gunshot is still ringing out in my mind. I wouldn't be able to hunt an animal, I'm incapable of it, and yet it's Zev's cowardice I denounce—the cowardice of a performer. Zev plays the rifle as Théo plays the piano. Their evasion is even more cowardly than the one I project for myself. It manifests as a failure, trapped in the illusion of a kind of purity, of justice. The piano's defilement is the same as the rifle's: instruments of execution, distance behind a mask. I'd rather stay lost. I'd still rather tear myself away than admire these gestures mechanically. My scorn, I never hid it from Zev: we were bound—he, Théo, and I—by a pact of demolition, reciprocal and uncompromising.

Blows bring us closer. Friendship as the voluntary confrontation of foreign bodies. Cannibalism is never far. I oscillated between the desire to kill them and the desire to be devoured, completely assimilated by Zev and Théo's bodies. Letting myself get snatched up by another appetite would have lent me a kind of power. I wasn't important enough for a sacrifice, however insane. My search for what to do invites me to become the carcass and the butcher at the same time, expediting the murders that have already been set into motion. For in this city of mutilated people who try to survive with their predictable renunciations, death is preceded by nothing other than a series of murders.

Striking a balance between disgust and the will for annihilation is delicate. If I want to absent myself instead of letting myself curdle, it's as public property, by insubordination, an act of refusal as absolute as it is unjustified.

*

Zev doesn't write me anymore. He doesn't write because nothing calls him back to me, and I won't write back because nothing calls me back to myself. He's clearly read his Stirner; he knows there comes a time when everyone knocks down their boundaries, and if he doesn't write back, it's because he doesn't feel like writing back, because he won't let himself get sucked in by the obligations of symmetry, of an equal distribution in correspondence.

May silence now scratch a line between our two voices, which Théo Schultz's privileged defenestration brought back into contact, briefly made to cross again.

*

With the help of the rogyapas, flesh torn from flesh is proffered to the carrion eaters and detritivores.

When the heart stops beating mid-fall, the body encounters its tomb in the sky.

The falling man, breaking against the world.

Falling; falling, like fire.

*

An outset, undone. The gesture never begun. Hastened by rage, I botch myself. The day stretches on without pause, the sun blanching everything around me. The cruel hours reveal to me other peoples' mores, their good conduct, a coherent, orderly disposition. I await the night, between the cry and the enclave, in a sort of limbic torpor. Domestication doesn't impose obedience: therein lies the possibility of resistance, but also the realization, usually resigned, of its difficulty. My fire will be another.

*

Garbage collector strike: a group crosses the Grande Place, demands government action. Their slogan, "What's the use?" spreads over the crowd with the animal blood. Trash piles up on sidewalks, roads, roofs; the meat, swallowing up everyday things while the flies buzz on like cars around a racetrack.

Disturbance. A naked man approaches the protestors, shouts, dances, shaking his soft arms, his filthy hair, his face split by a toothless smile. Some people walking by stop amusedly, holding up their screens, start recording and taking photos—a false complicity sets in. The cops show up in no time.

I look at their gloved hands, their polished billy clubs. Sir, you don't have the right to be naked in public. Sir, there are children present. Are you intoxicated? Sir. We're going to have to arrest you. You're under arrest. Come on now, let's go. Come with us. Don't make us cuff you. Come on, let's go have a word. The man explodes into laughter, continues his dance. Thinning patience gives the impression that devastation isn't far off. Sir. The man screams in anger, panics, tries to save himself. First blow: the establishment demands its threat, stability its violence, order its censorship.

The man turns towards me: and what about you, sister? Aren't you going to help me?

They take him downtown. The little crowd disperses. I hang back.

From here, I can see a bright strip. A few years ago, having found that the number of people throwing themselves off the Pont Central was too high, and having calculated the danger these falling bodies posed to the flow of traffic below the bridge, they assigned an unnamed architect the project of constructing a barrier of metal posts attached to each other with a mesh of barbed wire and luminescent fibers. The majority seems delighted by this construction's neat symbolism, the glow fending off the fatal action. It's the tyranny of light, the control of bodies by the obstruction of the fall.

I stuff my hand into my pocket. I tear up the newspaper with my fingernail.

Théo, disintegrated.

Think of the other children stuck behind in our country, think of the ones who didn't have your luck, we gave you this opportunity, we sacrificed ourselves for you, we still sacrifice ourselves every day, and this is how you thank us, how you show us your gratitude? What do you want, to come back, is that it? To come back to this shit? You think we have bottomless pockets, that we can pay for these plane tickets whenever you feel like it? We've had enough now, you have to get your act together. I hope you're saying your prayers every day. And that you're eating enough. It's not that bad, is it? Your uncle came by the house last night, I cooked him fish just the way you like it, and can you believe it, he refused to eat it, he thought it was going to make him sick, something about mercury! I'm telling you, the whole world's insane. You've got to stay strong. May God be with you, daughter; may he show you His light.

This cold that, as was once said, increases with brightness, signals an apocalyptic light that sterilizes any profusion of vital bacteria with its refrigeration. The grand finale will not be the chaotic and bloody one promised by the menace of holy imagery. It will be a rigorous cleansing, a systematic overexposure, a doctrine of traceability that takes the hazard out of ruin. The spaces have already been dissolved into divided territories. You can't even talk about disappointment anymore. The fascist hemorrhage controls the texture of forgetfulness, the maneuvering of the margins, the cartographies of flight.

I've heard enough talk about the Enlightenment, about the mind's clarity, lucidity, fire contained like a little bedside lamp, these histories that silence others, but my irritation mixes with the bursting roots of the oaks carefully spaced out along the sidewalks, the greenery calculated according to the neighborhood's value. They have to be destroyed, torn up from the earth, because there's no one left to assassinate, the decisions have been made, and every conspiracy is the work of some diffuse bureaucracy. Blank screens enable the uniformity of confiscation, profiling: I don't want to have to clarify or provide updates. I don't want a dissecting light, but the body's night, the night of apparition.

No salvation in mistrust, pruning isn't enough, beyond the fingernails broken by pigheaded digging, beyond the heart withered by staggered breath, there's still the certainty of the rain: I am listening. Breathing without waiting to feel the hollow pounding of what's tearing me apart— echoes and intervals dodge any possible identification, the kind I dispute to demolish the wall and save the window. Aborting myself, among the ranks, the capitulations, the capitals and capital.

The transparency of the game proposed and the negotiations it requires leave bruises under the skin, disarm my vigilance. Transfigurations: the instability of the envelope, of eye color, of skin, of facial features. I transform insanely fast—the world is what haunts me, my outstretched bones.

Self-immolation is the next step, the one that will leave no space for evolution, no form permitting a successful conclusion.

Neither search nor vagary: the gesture. The burning body falls by letting itself be seen, and despite the causes defended, despite the injunction, all that's left of the sacrifice is the freezeframe of its spectacle, an offering with neither giver nor receiver, the outline of an address to take or leave.

I will be the flaming horizon, the shore offering no welcome, the guttering cruelty of a distance made surface.

You're bored, little Narr. I'll tell you, you know, the war... those were the days. The shells gave us life, whistling over our heads, flying all over the place, we said we've got to have fun, make the most of life. What a party we had back then! War just isn't the same anymore. It's all attacks from planes, drones, mines forgotten underground or laid by extremists, those little conmen with their Kalashnikovs, and everyone claims they're fighting for God when they're only out to save their own skin. It's different now. Back then, and I'm talking about thirty years ago, everything still happened on the ground, on the street, you could feel the war on your way to school. It was exciting, all the girls didn't wait so long before they let you kiss them, everyone had their own gun, people were shooting everywhere, you could hear the shots at night, and the shouting. There were scary moments, for sure, I lost friends, my cousin, then my neighbor who got cut down when he was out looking for diapers for his baby. But even with all that, when I hear you talking I realize those were the golden days. We didn't have electricity at our marriages, we did our chores by candlelight, we had to boil water whenever we wanted to take a bath, it was an adventure just going out for groceries. Now the whole world's within easy reach, it's too easy, there's no more struggle. What do you want, you've got to live while you're young. Did you find a job? Your mother's worried, you know. Are you looking, at least? It's been a good month, business was great, I'm going to send you some cash, it makes me happy to help you.

The minks released from the fur factory obviously died in our hostile forests, just like the elephant who escaped only to get slaughtered in the middle of the highway, the emaciated toucans kidnapped by the Army for Animals.

I cash out. It would be better to put my money elsewhere, to deposit funds, but I don't trust any group. There's always the need to be governed or the repetition of what we dispute, the exclusions, the hierarchies, the tyrannical resentments. Nowhere to run, no departure. No more radicals: just heads full of bramble, accolades, and name-dropping. We talk about nature. We chop things down. The monolithic construction plops itself down on the black waters.

Free the dogs!

All I'd need is a tank of gas to work up the courage to immolate myself for no apparent reason. An incandescent, combustible acceleration.

This action will only be possible on the condition of its being seen. The horror I've caused in other people is all I'll have to help me endure a pain that will only go away, according to my research, once the fire breaches my nervous system. But to decide on one gaze means to decide on a place that risks being associated with a cause. They'll try to make sense of it, nothing will be taken as random.

I'd have to graft a message onto the thing itself, something like "I refuse" or, to cut to the chase, just "no." But still, nothing's certain: these vultures will do anything to establish coherency. They'll say I'm mentally unstable, they'll talk about women, the economy, or immigration. But no, really, short of writing a manifesto—best not to make a scene. Maybe go about it impulsively. After all, I have nothing to say.

★

The fed-up citizens pour gas over their trash while the oil companies conspire up north. They promise the gagged populations economic electroshock. From now on, any resistance is an attack on the national body.

We draw the blinds, lock our doors, build barriers between our houses. We sculpt our shrubbery and mow our lawns. Our faces contort, full of mistrust, ready to fink for the ransom.

Fruit pickers head west, others stick around in order to sink deep into the swampy forests, where, training their endurance amidst swarms of mosquitos, they'll plant trees whose lot is to be cut down. A profitable symbiosis, paid by the seed, which will help them pay off their student debt before they end up homeless.

Tourist season is around the bend: on the newspaper stands, in front of the vacation rentals, and in the restaurants, they raise colorful banners in commemoration of the self-proclaimed discoverers of these lands. They announce, on the radio, a variety of events: folk concerts, excursions, and guided visits to villages that reenact the olden days, the zoo's reopening. Rhinos, kangaroos, hippos, and parrots arrive on freighters.

Some people flagellate themselves along the roads, their shirts torn and soaked with blood. They look skyward, and appear to be happy.

They have declared, in the infected zones, a halt in construction. The sites will be abandoned for an indeterminate amount of time, despite the prospective tenants' impatience. To avoid squatting and vandalism, the entrepreneurs have taken recourse to maximum security: guards make their rounds through the unfinished skeletons of the buildings that, during this interim, will remain untouched.

Behind the plastic membrane enclosing the restaurant's patio, a man is busy wiping the tables with a rag to clear them of crumbs, while a woman dawdles about, her thumb pressed to her lips, hesitating before the dessert menu. She chooses a pear tart, which arrives, glistening with pectin.

*

My father calls me again. He claims to have found a solution to my problem: a distant cousin works in the kitchen at an old folk's home, and he could make some introductions for me there, at least get me an interview. You know him, Anouar, well, come on, don't you remember, when you were little? I gave him your number, he'll be calling you soon.

ANOUAR

Narr, my dear, I'm so happy to lend a hand! I have so many fond memories of you, you know, you were such a little troublemaker, always something to say! Now, your father told me about your situation and it's perfect timing. There are some interviews taking place next week, and I recommended you. I told them you had cleaning experience from back home, they never check when it's foreign work. All you have to do is drop off your papers, they'll call you if they hang on to your application. Between you and me, it should be simple. I heard they're really hurting for employees, and with my good word, you're a shoo-in. But hey, you could give a call every now and then, you've got my number now, come by the house for dinner sometime!

I hear a weird noise, a kind of rubbing. Hunched over at the foot of a tree, a man appears to be masturbating. Others pretend not to notice, they cast each other scandalized glances, consolidating their normalcy as they check to see if there are hidden cameras in the bushes to broadcast their reaction for the amusement of lonesome retirees.

Where does this sudden urge to remove my sex come from? Right now, my only ambition is to get kidnapped and tortured, but the chances are slim. I'm unable to keep quiet, to stop thinking about the same images, the same sentences, like an old haunted house that doesn't scare anyone anymore. This isn't failure: I'm not actually trying to do anything.

Bits of lard dangle from the branches, swaying, poised to fall. The rats sniff at them and run away, aghast. They stick to the trunks, quiet as lizards, the nervous beating of their bodies is all that betrays their presence.

This walk in the park is like every walk, this park like every park, this city like every city. I get stuck, the earth swallowing its rotten slop under each of my footsteps. I bend down and push my hands into the grass, which instantly decomposes as my fingers sink into a moist warmth. I dig.

The hole becomes enormous, revealing worms, roots, and wet rocks. Soon enough they'll be asking me to explain myself, but for now they're happy just to speed up a little whenever they walk past me. I dig, and the very act of digging brings me a ridiculous sense of comfort.

★

Memory of luxury, of spacious rooms, fine dining, pastries, sugarcoated walnuts, lime-glazed macarons, strawberries injected with champagne, braised lamb served on a bed of tagliatelle and spritzed with truffle oil, all this swishing together now in this dirty bucket with the built-in strainer where I put the mop, twist it, and wipe it over the tiling at the nursing home, where the old folks have their own stubborn memories, their impressions ingrained though often hard to locate, their diffuse anxiety, which they cradle while stirring amorphous purees on plastic plates, coming and going in the hallways, waiting for something that will never come, shitting pure liquid and holding onto a sandblasted handrail I sterilize twice a day with an unidentified chemical product.

I don't clean surfaces but consciences, so the old folks won't get sick, so they can continue to occupy their beds, so their families will know that we're watching over them, that they're safe in a home fully adapted to their needs. There's a woman who screams, screams all the time, they move her to the sun lounge, to the cafeteria, to her room, but she keeps screaming, everywhere and always with the same terror, the same accusation. They're always adjusting her prescriptions, they give her sedatives, but she screams, sometimes a little less loudly, from a little further away, depending on the dose. For the most part the others are silent, they mumble, look around, greet the employees by nodding their heads, they ask the time, the day of the week, and lie down again, surrounded by their things, photos of their grandchildren, empty vases, crucifixes.

Sometimes I want to choke them, break their bones, make their degeneration visible by accelerating the violence of this place. I do my job, I take my breaks, I eat my sandwich, go back upstairs, finish my rounds, make my pay, and feign gratitude. Every day is visiting day, yet visitors are rare.

They want to leave as soon as they arrive, come around mostly at mealtime to spoonfeed their parents and lay out plates and empty little jars on the table. It gives them a set time limit, the meal, a time slot, an excuse to go running off.

I always save the same room to clean last. In the golden light of the late afternoon I gather myself in this enormous space, which could easily house four or five residents, but there are only two, a couple, Mr. and Mrs. Y., as indicated by the little plaque tacked up on their door. Their beds are arranged to face each other. They sleep constantly, fed by nasogastric tubes. Their life support systems pump in counterpoint. I dust around the plastic orchids left out on Mr. Y.'s bedside table. His face is a disastrous fruit, a yellow, marbled skin with dead veins, burst blood vessels, divided by a half-open eye that always seems to be watching me.

Ever since I took up my noble post as a housekeeping employee, I have touched my possessed body constantly, this territory occupied at every point of flesh. My orgasms are only mine in the blinding glare that precedes my collapse. Like a junkie, I masturbate behind the parked cars, squatting down among the overflowing trash cans, or crossing my legs to the point of cumming in the waiting rooms of the oncology department, where the conversations between strangers are overbearing, despite the magazines and Muzak they have on offer. At work, I touch myself in the filthiest, saddest places, the places that turn me on most: in a blind man's room, behind the curtain, and sometimes in the storage closet, facing the solvent bottles, the rolls of absorbent toilet paper, the boxes of latex gloves, and the rags folded and stacked according to their size, raising my head occasionally to stare at the greenish mold growing around the air duct. When I cum, my hatred shatters into mottos.

toxic smells
we wash our houses, we wash our cities
we scrub, we shine, we dust to forget
the invisible maids help us forget
nothing but a mess left behind in a plastic bucket
cleaning is a sanitary act
cleaning is a social structure
cleaning is an act of preservation
preservation is always a form of destruction
the death of 99% of germs is a value
the containers say: Pure Spring, Ocean Breeze, Pine Forest
I'm going to puke.

★

I work the same shift as a woman named Malika. Malika
calls me Nour, even though I repeatedly tell her my name
is Narr, it just doesn't make sense to her, she hears Nour,
light. She also comes from somewhere else, too, she tells me
she's saving up, but absolutely not to go back to her home
country. I confess my royal childhood to her, tell her my
memories of the castle, and she sweeps them all away with
a wave of her hand, tells me to get over my nostalgia, it
won't do me any good. "Little Nour, that's just childhood
speaking. Childhood always exaggerates, and you'd be
disappointed to see what's left of it, I'm sure, even if I've
never seen your house. I went back to my parents' one time,
they'd gotten old, they were all wrinkly, the house and the
garden, too, everything had shrunken, it was all so sad!
Believe me, it's better to stay here with your memories."
I love when she calls me "Little Nour," I feel like a little
firefly in her forest. I imagine that she's hiding, close to

her skin, under the smell of latex and solvents, an orange blossom scent.

"I don't think it's because of childhood."

"No use pretending for me. I know how shameful it feels to lie, and when you hear them talk, you'd think every immigrant was a noble back in their country. It makes you wonder why they come here at all."

Maybe the whole world is withering away, that must be it, the impression of something narrowing, of an increasingly restrained, if not impossible, freedom of movement, and I'm not just talking about surveillance.

Work adapts to the tyranny of light—one erosion summons the next. I cohere in the darkness, the day and I having nothing to offer each other. So it's not exactly I who am washing the nursing home floor, but my spectral body, heavy as sleep and practically transparent. The night drugs me, easing the hours. Now it's harder, because I have to get up early. One day, I won't go to work, I'll calmly let myself get fired, even though I dare to hope for an earthquake.

*

Shrapnel memories, scarified architectures.

Others, like me, left the colonies, injecting a bit of capital into air commerce, the sky's filth. They flee the war, dream through their children. Follow trails, cross paths again from time to time. Connected: often they speak several cities in the same breath. They recognize each other, start communities of exiles and expats. Cyborg bodies, projected backward.

Out there, over here. In the promised land, we specialize under the pretext of flourishing, fighting what haunts us, silently passing the obstruction, through our searching, of possibilities rendered unrecognizable.

Departure is a separation. Leaving, breaking into parts.

Division: totalitarian rigging, the illusion of assemblage, the elimination of noise.

Today I feel like a warrior, unpredictable and interstitial: a separation that can't occur until there are neither divisions nor places.

We need soldiers, Zev said. We have to join forces.

But the warrior is not a soldier. She doesn't take orders: obedience is unknown to her. She knows that every cause has already been lost.

Combat is elsewhere.

THE HORIZON IS BURNING

To commit one's crime and assume one's
participation in the darkness of the world.

FELWINE SARR

The desire to leave comes before the leaving. Despite the fires, despite the houses in ruins, we always end up somewhere, with our own pollution stuck to our bodies, the ruminated garbage, the colonial dream of an enchanted forest. Maps don't account for every border: from afar, territories look hollowed out, like carcasses prepped for the market. And Zev can't distinguish the marks of ownership upon them: places, to him, appear vast and mysterious, like promises of freedom. He doesn't dare imagine the forest, and hastily awaits a landscape insensitive to the abstract nature of his combat. It's only in coming closer that he notices the compartments, the zones that have been divvied up again and again, the shores of shared lakes, the lands saturated with wheat, framed by electric fences, the road signs and names of little country roads that arrogantly denote what was destroyed in order to clear their place: Chemin du Marécage, Allée des Renards Blancs, Birch Lane, Caribou Street.

*

Théo waiting aboard the plane taking him to the Old Country, Narr plunging her hands into a bucket of soapy water, Zev accelerating at the wheel of a stolen van: their anachronistic trajectories freeze-frame there at the final compromise. The age of power has ended, bodies resolved to find a path have let the implicit peaks of their ambitions dampen down. For a time, the three of them had whispered of their belief in a destiny that would occur regardless of their existence, that would come to catch them amidst whatever choices they had weighed: this inoffensive mediocrity was the risk of a reasonable mourning. Their potential had carved out the space for a corresponding deflation.

★

Zev never mentioned he was leaving, but he let it be understood, he couldn't help it. Coy, even in his protest. He bought what he needed, impossible to steal in those stores. He made his selections, carried out the transactions, armed himself and stashed the necessary materials away. He trained. He read, practiced, learned.

Now it has to be forgotten.

No more rage, slogans, poems.

Along the paths, climbing plants already have the cars in their grip, like rusty shipwrecks, abandoned by individuals or families who tried to escape through the woods. In the ghost towns, a number of cow carcasses still decompose in the sunlight. The inspectors have been systematic: a single cow is enough to represent a threat to public health, so every breeder is responsible for the slaughter of his entire lot of cows if even one presents symptoms. Some of the farmers had dug in their heels and refused, so the inspectors showed up in person, pistols in hand. They looked like ghosts, in their plastic raincoats and particle masks covering the bottom half of their faces.

They say bison haunt these places, that their tubercular phantoms wander here without relief, and, beside them, those of Indian vultures, executed circus animals, hanged elephants.

Zev steps over the cadavers and walks toward oblivion.

He's ready for the war.

★

The war won't be declared.

As soon as the ferry disembarks he feels it, the ineluctable residue of what he's leaving behind. On the deck, a dozen or so parked cars. Some people are napping inside them, others stretch their legs, watching the island approach. Escape already has the aftertaste of an encroachment on a mute and demanding cruelty.

Bathing in the gentle sea spray on the deck, certain passengers watch Zev, at first subtly, then with a disturbing, irresistible insistence. His beauty is impossible to overlook. A man with a shaved head and arms covered in tattoos approaches him. He offers to let him in: no way he'll catch the next ferry on foot. Zev politely declines. Jilted, the man goes and sits back down in his car.

The moment they dock at the wharf, the cars start up and parade down the main street. Slow and massive, the ferry turns around. Zev lingers on the docks amidst the smells of gas and saltwater. The sound of the motors fades, clearing the air for the stubborn cries of a blue jay, a repetitive song, something like the creaking of a rusty swing.

*

The trees no longer bear fruit and the earth is dry, as if the tide had risen here to sow its salts. Black sap and bramble intertwine, nests fall from the balding branches, parasites dig their furrows into the wet trunks, and birches shed their rotting bark. The forest is slowly collapsing.

One is alone in the forest, and everything inside the body tries to escape this solitude. Zev thinks he sees a few posters, signs, and billboards, which disappear as soon as he approaches them. The city has trained his eye.

He walks in ever deeper to forget, to survive, so everything will mix together and start moving again, but everything ingrained in him explodes in a larval proliferation with every unknotted muscle, every resounding pain, the dropped guard of those cottony nights. The bodies he has known cling to his skin, track him down while he destroys, under his steps, the glaucous sculptures of lichen. He isn't moving away from anything at all.

★

Zev spares us the sight of his fall.

He won't come back. By this spectacular diffraction, resistance becomes flight and courage, cowardice. Zev goes in deeper, letting his myth hang suspended, a name whispered around the bonfire. He leaves us to our storyteller anecdotes, he leaves us to our language and walks on to dislodge his gaze.

Beyond the hiking trails, at the deepest point of the forest, are the piercing howls of the chainsaws. The planes still glide overhead. Their plaint mixes with the hum of the endlessly struggling flies caught in his hair, stuck in the folds of his ears. The forest guts him, his ravaged skin swells, hardened by countless bites. At first he shakes his head, his arms, but his sweat only attracts further hungry insects who tear off little bits of his flesh, sucking his blood and injecting their poisons. He sees he can't fight them and grows used to the burn, as constant as wrath. His blood courses through other bodies, circulates throughout their frenetic reproduction, their gorged organs that will be devoured by others, curdleing in decomposed carcasses and rising up once again into the foliage, everything aswarm in one great rape.

That's when something else pierces the air, first with the sweet persistence of tinnitus. A buzzing, more invasive than even the mosquitos', amplifies without end.

The strength of the noise is such that it quickly becomes impossible to tell if it's coming from the core of the earth, from the sky, or from his own gut. It carries the indifferent memories of those who came before, of tanks, highways, sirens, and sonar.

The birds have taken flight in a sudden start, everything that can either falls or breaks away, the rest jolts to the point of cracking. The perforated eardrum has unveiled a trembling labyrinth through which Zev staggers, too shaken for terror.

This surpasses disfigurement. There's nothing left to recognize.

★

Here they pump water, the mountains go dry and the pine needles pile up on the ground. Sometimes the fires are caused by lightning, but more often by the negligence of campers who bury their coals carelessly or the greed of landowners who raze their run-down houses in hopes of collecting on insurance.

Kneeling at the far end of the island, Zev watches the burning horizon.

The red tide rises, gorged with toxic oysters. The ocean moans. Zev looks over translucent piles of crustaceans, the flashing scales of herring and salmon regurgitated by the water, the slow implosion of young belugas beached on the pebbles.

Cold, already. Zev stands up, stretches, something comes apart in his hips, a thick, gelatinous mass rises up to his throat.

The wood cracks, the thujas pitch like algae, the wolves howl, and the helicopters fly off toward the fire. Amidst the smoke, they'll speak of mobilization, economic losses, criminal investigation. They'll say: no matter what, you can't fight evil with evil.

The unpredictability of the fires is enchanting. After the spectacle, arrests will be made to the fullest extent of the law.

Such momentum will pass, brought back to the order of a sedimented principle. We'll forget.

Then comes the thirst. The sweep of a bare domestication, a momentary stupefaction. We will await a punishment, some resolution, but there will be nothing beside this thirst and its scream—the plenitude of its scream.

FIRES——NARR SINGS

in the end
it must
be completely dark
even the emergency exit must be turned off
completely dark
absolutely dark

THOMAS BERNHARD

When the Joelma Building catches fire in downtown São Paulo, and the people stuck inside start throwing themselves out the windows to escape the flames, the crowd's inability to help is what pardons its gaze. Unlike in the cases of Dziekanski or the photograph of the vulture eyeing the starving child, the one who takes the picture, confronted with the body falling from up high, is not condemned for his observation, his decision not to intervene.

"...*money!!!...I am haunted*," wrote Kevin Carter before gassing himself in his car after receiving the Pulitzer.

★

Narr doesn't exist.
Narr is taking a walk in the park.
The meat rises.
The man rises and falls before Théo's eyes.
Théo falls into the gaze.
The gaze forgets, drains out.
The gaze devours, holds tight, lets go.
Théo
Théo will not play anymore.
Théo has never played.
Théo plays out.
In the picture of the fall, Théo is playing out.
Théo's fall, then, is a sacrifice.
No.
Théo's fall is an offering to the martyrs.
The forgetful martyrs.
Théo offers himself up, while he falls and the meat rises.
It's always the same man falling. Always the same body.
The same fall in what it provokes.

Narr refuses.

Narr is no martyr.

She witnesses nothing.

She says: I am the fire. I am the attack.

Théo saw the fire.

The falling man is falling because he saw the fire.

There is the fall and there is the repetition of the fall.

The martyr multiplied by his viewing of the fall.

Of the body interrupted, the suspended image.

Pressing pause doesn't capture the fall.

The fall is the rejected image.

The falling body rejects itself.

Lets itself be taken.

Engulfed.

For the gaze.

And the gaze swallows.

The hungry gaze won't let go.

The gaze cuts into the falling man's flesh.

The gaze is a fire that one approaches

in order to fall.

*

Up until the last moment, digitized melodies of prior centuries associate suburban boredom with a commercial liberation in the arcades. Nostalgic hymns console the abulic, their palliative accessibility subject to a castrating maintenance, the delimitation of the accessibility of desires, angers, hopes, and maladies. We'll soon move on to some other self, flashing games and bells that inject brief thrills of incremental victory, immediate chemical gratification.

Up until the very last moment, behind the glass walls, agitators move their lips and play the markets, bowing in front of columns of screens where shifting numbers have replaced the oracles. Their borrowed gestures, like those of ballerinas, link them to a small, easily identifiable group, the guarantee of a tradition that serves as an alibi for their white knuckles, closed tight around the handles of their briefcases.

*

After the fracas, the elements spin out in incalculable directions. After the fracas, the important thing is not what remains but what can explode, what has been waiting to give in. Such is what friction enables.

Narr. Propulsion of particles toward the light, a form of aleatory saltation, which traverses while being traversed. Which would allow for an embrasure. The echo of a color, the breadth of an oscillation. A gesture that wouldn't exist if not for its impact. A window without a wall. A movement beyond dance. Beyond matter, the indeterminate passage of a vibration to undo the unity of forms: a circulation outside of any market.

*

The children play, running in front of broken fire hydrants, facing staircases that open out onto the foundations of their ruined houses, they laugh, soaked, their see-through clothes sticking to their skin and warming the hearts of the old, sometimes rapacious folks who amble by with their empty, creaky shopping carts. When the waters lose their twilit gilding, the children scatter in packs and leave the stragglers to get snatched up by the cars of breakaways or by trembling hands grasping at softness. They remember forbidden words, orders to disobey. They make love in the night, their teeth rotten from sugar, their hands stained with dirt. They chase rats and sleep in the trash cans where they find the things they use to build their kingdoms. They adopt one-eyed kittens, wingless pigeons, which they cuddle before snapping their necks.

★

Underground rumblings, a long dormant stratification. Something magnetic rises up, seismic variations resound in the golden moles' thin eardrums. The architecture hesitates in tunnels, rain patters on loose tiles, constructions lean over, and wild cats shriek with hunger in the anticipated rubble.

Narr walks, streets pass by and cars rust in place, the letters of the Hotel Jéricho cave in, the Ryōunkaku Tower gives way again and again, passersby applaud and watch the wrinkling faces and thinning hands in shock. The bodies crumple, then melt, boneless on the sidewalks, their belts and shoes falling to pieces shortly thereafter. The sand sneaks in under the doors, through the houses' cracks. Libraries become dunes; kitchens, deserts; bedrooms, mausoleums.

★

The wind, in gusts, dishevels the city, scatters the ashes of hens, thorns, flowers, and seeds. Hermaphroditic bouquets of primrose and asclepia blanket the rotten meat and burnt trash. Surrounded by wheat, cedar roots break through the roads. Creepers, bougainvilleas, honeysuckles, and hydrangeas weave together, unbolt the locks, block the windows, crush the chimneys' bricks. Foxes climb yipping out from the earth, throw themselves on the debris, and scratch off what's left of the wallpaper. The city grinds like a foundering ship, resuscitated crows and blue jays chatter festively atop the plane trees, while the palms and baobabs explode as quickly as shells, destroying the surrounding asphalt.

Narr is not alone. There is Théo's ghost, and Zev's, there's the Ryōunkaku Tower falling, righting itself, and falling again like one great sonic pulse. There are flies and these tables where one can still hear phantoms discussing profitability.

The sun jumps with a start, elongating shadows go into a panic, no longer obey a thing. The bells are ringing but there's no one left to pray, no one left to hear the prayers. The final faith is a vortex, an incantation swept into itself. The ringing wanders off, the light falls frenetically. The convulsive slackening. At dawn the birds declare their survival, and the falling man keeps falling in the city dissected piece by piece.

*

Narr sings without words.

From her stomach, from her sex, from her throat she sings the disaster, the wordless fire. She sings the body lost, quartered between continents, the dying reef, the dying ocean, the animals, the gunshot. A form thrashing on the water's dark surface.

Narr vibrates, resounds. She sings to the bottom of the Earth. The bottom of the Earth sings in Narr. All that is spoken sings through her.

Narr sings as the dogs howl. Her voice is beautiful and warm, the body of a bird, a faraway city flashing in the night.

She escapes, but to nowhere: the windows are open because the doors are always closed.

This singing goes unheard, it breaks from harmony. There's no precision. No memory of singing. Nothing in it is honed.

Narr sings, erases, forgets her forgetting. She sings to avoid naming, to avoid the murder that is speech.

★

Time now to slide under the earth, into the entrails of a clotted architecture. There, we dance in the tunnels, beat out rhythms against the walls, burn linens to rekindle the heat of the coals piled on the railroad tracks. Everyone cries out in their language, and every language is foreign. Voices linger in echoes, impossible to tell where they came from. We fight amongst ourselves, we kill without interference. Between the bricks there perspires a rancid water, hollowing out the fissures that, according to some, lead on to another world: many study these black cracks and try to find a light inside, like the mad pyrite lovers of old.

People walking by whisper their prices, accustomed to discretion, despite the absence of law in these places. They claim to know of paths one can take to thriving cities, to country fields where fruits still grow, and try in vain to gather groups of travelers who would dare dream of setting out again. Uselessly, we keep our money in our pockets, in case it could serve some use: some still believe in the possibility of a return to order. On improvised stages, past lives are dictated in laments—all recount and none listens. These declamations console the one delivering them, like the compulsive cradling of lonely bodies, the twitching of faces tinted blue by screen light.

Narr moves on, in search of an astonishment that never comes. Everything is familiar to her, she knows all too well what preceded these residues. So, she sings. She sings as she awaits the rain that will come to wash it all away, to break the places she will flee when the next earthquake hits, while drunken bodies nod off to sleep, guided toward each other in spite of themselves. She keeps her eyes out for some inhabited place, stumbles endlessly into little gatherings, hostile circles that remind her she has nothing to offer but this frozen song, these melodies of stupefaction. It would take finding some other way, a ladder, climbing out from a sewer drain onto the abandoned surface.

★

An outset, an urge, undone.
Narr abolishes herself, squanders herself with no return.
She vomits, stuffed, starts again, vomits history, dances like that, not looking for anything anymore. Says: everything that passes through me is possessed. Can't say I anymore. Can't want anymore. Broken. Nothing. Without violence. Collapse. Not even a failure. Not even a loss.
The city has been destroyed, abandoned.
Narr is the city, destroyed and abandoned. No desire or revolution.

Rush. A cry in the empty city, the body empty.

Languageless writing. Between.

Narr will admit nothing. The silence of song.

The falling man keeps falling.

The falling man is free.

The falling man's freedom is not the freedom of a sovereign body, but an offering's.

No.

No more freedom, no more imprisonment.

A dance, a song as offering.

Fire: between the lip and the tooth, a placeless fire, a madness's motion, fire's insanity.

Leaving, running in place, like the falling man. Falling like fire.

★

The great showers have begun to fall, rising waters carry the cities' excrements in rivers across the highways, the bridges' alveoli clogged with trash and meat.

Wandering, the body soaked beyond the body.

From impasse to impasse, Narr sings with the rain birds, sings blindly all the way to the forest stripped by the waters in which she steps over broken branches, the corpses of drowned mammals, abandoned tarps, and collapses, disarmed, the moment the world astounds itself by becoming music.

ACKNOWLEDGMENTS

The author and translator would like to thank Nathanaël for being attentive and present throughout the making of this book, both in French and in English; Judah Rubin and Ben Schluter for their input on the translation; as well as Caelan, Gia, Jaye, Lindsey, Stephen, and the entire Nightboat team for welcoming these voices and ruins.

OLIVIA TAPIERO is a writer and translator. She has published *Les murs* (2009), *Espaces* (2012), *Phototaxie* (2017), and *Rien du tout* (2021), and has co-edited *Chairs* (2019). She lives in Tio'tia:ke (Montréal).

KIT SCHLUTER is author of *Pierrot's Fingernails* and *5 Cartoons*. He has translated numerous books from the French and Spanish, and edited *The Beauty Salons: Writers & Poetas at Aeromoto 2017-2020*. He lives in Mexico City.

NIGHTBOAT BOOKS

Nightboat Books, a nonprofit organization, seeks to develop audiences for writers whose work resists convention and transcends boundaries. We publish books rich with poignancy, intelligence, and risk. Please visit nightboat.org to learn about our titles and how you can support our future publications.

The following individuals have supported the publication of this book. We thank them for their generosity and commitment to the mission of Nightboat Books:

Kazim Ali
Anonymous (4)
Abraham Avnisan
Jean C. Ballantyne
The Robert C. Brooks Revocable Trust
Amanda Greenberger
Rachel Lithgow
Anne Marie Macari
Elizabeth Madans
Elizabeth Motika
Thomas Shardlow
Benjamin Taylor
Jerrie Whitfield & Richard Motika

This book is made possible, in part, by grants from the New York City Department of Cultural Affairs in partnership with the City Council and the New York State Council on the Arts Literature Program.